03/04

I'LL FLY MY OWN PLANE

JEAN ALICIA ELSTER

ILLUSTRATED BY
NICOLE TADGELL

JUDSON PRESS ■ VALLEY FORGE

To my father, Norman V. Fuqua,
a proud veteran of World War II
(Master Sergeant, U.S. Army),
and my mother, Jean Ford Fuqua —JAE

Very special thanks to Mark Tadgell,
my husband and my friend, with his great
collection of WWII books and expertise.
Love and hugs, Nickie

I'LL FLY MY OWN PLANE

The Scripture on page 3 is quoted from HOLY BIBLE: *New International Version*, copyright 8 1973, 1978, 1984. Used by permission of Zondervan Bible Publishers. Joe Joe's library book, *Tuskegee Airmen: Flying for Freedom*, is a fictional publication. The information attributed to that book was gleaned from the following sources: Charles E. Francis, *The Tuskegee Airmen: The Men Who Changed a Nation*, 4th ed. (Boston: Branden Publishing Company, 1997); Alan L. Gropman, *The Air Force Integrates, 1945-1964*, 2nd ed. (Washington, D.C.: Smithsonian Institution Press, 1998); Lawrence P. Scott and William M. Womack Sr., *Double V: The Civil Rights Struggle of the Tuskegee Airmen* (East Lansing, Mich.: Michigan State University Press, 1994); NASA Quest website: http://quest.arc.nasa.gov/qchats/special/mlk00/afam_astronauts.html. Vintage photos by Bettman / Corbis. Astronaut photos by Roger Ressmeyer / Corbis.

Library of Congress Cataloging-in-Publication Data
Elster, Jean Alicia.
   I'll Fly My Own Plane / Jean Alicia Elster ; illustrated by Nicole Tadgell.
   p.cm. — (Joe Joe in the city)
SUMMARY: Joe Joe is tempted to earn "easy money" drug running like his friend Tyrone, but reading about the Tuskegee Airmen helps him decide what he should do. ISBN 0-8170-1407-1 (alk. paper)
   [1. Conduct of life—Fiction. 2. African Americans—Fiction. 3. Air pilots—Fiction. 4. United States. Army Air Forces. Fighter Group, 332nd—Fiction.] I. Tadgell, Nicole, 1969- ill. II. Title. III. Series.
PZ7 .E529 Il 2002
[Fic]—dc21   2002276243
Printed in China.

09 08 07 06 05 04 03 02
10 9 8 7 6 5 4 3 2 1

Whether you turn to the right or to the left, your ears will hear a voice behind you, saying, "This is the way; walk in it."
—Isaiah 30:21

Only Joe Joe Rawlings seemed to notice the sound of the jet plane high in the air above them. He stopped and looked up, watching the plane creep across the sky and knowing that it was really speeding along at hundreds of miles per hour. Then, realizing that Tyrone and Kalia had kept on walking, he ran to catch up with them.

"You're doing *what?*" Joe Joe asked, just hearing the end of what Tyrone was saying.

"I said I'm runnin' for Cecil now. I go by there after school," Tyrone explained. "And it's easy money. You should check it out, man. Go by and talk to him."

"*Talk* to him? I'm not even supposed to *walk* by his house," Joe Joe cringed.

"Me neither, Tyrone," Kalia added, shaking her head fiercely.

"What's wrong with you two?" Tyrone asked. He stopped walking and frowned at both of them. They were standing just a few yards from the library. "You should see what I bought with the money I made last week!" Tyrone bragged. "You'll never make this kind of money working for old Mr. Booth once a week like you do," Tyrone sneered at Joe Joe.

Joe Joe looked away with a shrug and saw his friend Mrs. Morgan, the librarian, standing at the front door of the library.

"Hey, you guys," Joe Joe said, turning back to face Tyrone and Kalia, "I need to run into the library and get a book. You wanna come in with me?"

"Naw, man." Tyrone started backing away. "Cecil's probably lookin' for me right now."

"Sorry, Joe Joe. Not today," Kalia replied quietly. "My baby sister's sick. I told my mom I'd be home on time today to help around the house." She waved to Joe Joe and then followed Tyrone down the sidewalk.

Mrs. Morgan held the door open for Joe Joe as he jogged up the library steps. "I saw you watching that jet as it flew overhead," she mentioned as they walked inside. "You like airplanes, don't you?"

"Sure do," Joe Joe answered eagerly as he followed her to her desk.

Mrs. Morgan reached over to a pile of books lying next to her computer. She picked up the top one. "Then here's a book I think you'll like," she smiled, handing it to him. When she saw Joe Joe frowning at the cover, Mrs. Morgan added, "It's pronounced Tuss-KEEG-ee."

"*Tuskegee Airmen: Flying for Freedom,*" Joe Joe read the title out loud. "Tuskegee Airmen?" he repeated.

"They were a very special group of African American pilots who flew planes for the United States Air Force during World War II," Mrs. Morgan explained. She squeezed Joe Joe's shoulder and added, "I think you'll like their story."

"Thanks, Mrs. Morgan." He waved as he walked eagerly over to the counter to check out the book.

When Joe Joe got home, he headed straight for the kitchen. "Hi, Grandma! Any cookies?" Joe Joe asked. His grandmother was standing by the stove with big oven mitts on her hands.

"Aren't there always?" she responded with a smile. "I'm just about to pull a fresh batch out of the oven. Go wash your hands. By the time you get back, I'll have them on the table."

Joe Joe dropped his school bag on the floor and put his library book on the kitchen table. He spotted his little brother playing under the table and bent down to grin at him. "Hi, Brandon!" he said and playfully tapped him on the nose. Then he noticed one of his mother's nurse's uniforms folded across a kitchen chair.

"Is Mom home?" he asked his grandmother.

Grandma shook her head. "No. She just left for work a few minutes ago."

"What about Dad? Is he home yet?"

"Yes, he's in the garage. But don't go out there."

"Why not?" Joe Joe asked curiously.

"He has his welding equipment out. He's working on some kind of surprise," she explained.

Joe Joe grinned when he heard the word *surprise*. Then he went to the bathroom and washed his hands.

Joe Joe was sitting at the kitchen table eating a cookie when his father came in through the back door. Mr. Rawlings still had on his welder's hood, eye goggles, and the big leather gloves that covered most of his arms.

Before Joe Joe could say hi, Brandon let out a yell from under the table and ran to hide behind his grandmother.

"Brandon," Mr. Rawlings called out, lifting his hood, "it's me, Daddy!"

Brandon peeked out from behind his grandmother as his father removed his goggles.

"Da-dee," he cried and ran toward his father. Quickly, Mr. Rawlings pulled off his gloves and swooped him up into the air.

Joe Joe and Grandma were laughing as Mr. Rawlings put Brandon back down on the floor. Then Joe Joe asked, still grinning, "What are you making, Dad? Can I come out and watch?"

"No, not this time," his father answered.

"Aw, Dad...."

"Patience, Joe Joe. It'll be worth the wait, I promise you," Dad reassured him. His father noticed the library book on the kitchen table. "Tuskegee Airmen, huh?" He gave Joe Joe's nose a tweak and went back out to the garage with one of Grandma's cookies in his hand and a sly grin on his face.

Chapter 2

"Yep, Tuskegee Airmen," Joe Joe repeated as he pulled the book toward him and opened it to the first page. He crunched happily on a cookie as he began to read.

The story of the Tuskegee Airmen—the African American pilots who flew in World War II—did not begin in 1942, the year that the first black graduates from U.S. Air Force pilot training received their "wings."

Nor did their story begin in 1932 when J. Herman Banning and Thomas Allen became the first African Americans to fly an airplane across the entire United States.

It did not even begin in 1929 with the opening of the first flying club for black pilots. (The other flying clubs admitted white members only.)

The beginnings of the Tuskegee Airmen can be traced to two African American pioneers in the field of aviation....

All of a sudden, Joe Joe heard a loud buzzing and whirring sound coming from the field behind his house. He looked up from his book. His grandmother was already looking out the kitchen window. "What is that?" he cried out, but Grandma was just shaking her head.

Leaving his grandmother at the kitchen window, Joe Joe ran outside. He saw his father through the open garage door, bending down over a piece of metal with the bright blue flame from his welding torch hissing. Dad hadn't noticed the noise. But Joe Joe saw what was happening. It was Tyrone and his newest toy.

THE TUSKEGEE AIRMEN
OF
WORLD WAR II
IN HONOR OF THE TUSKEGEE AIRMEN
THEIR INSTRUCTORS

These men were with the 99th U.S. Fighter Squadron, the first all-black outfit in the U.S. Air Force to take part in World War II.

Joe Joe ran to the field. Tyrone was holding the remote-control box for a model airplane. As Tyrone pushed the buttons and levers, the brown plane glided and dipped and sped through the air.

"Where did you get that?" Joe Joe asked Tyrone, raising his voice so he could be heard above the noise. Both boys had their eyes glued to the plane.

"I bought it with the money I made from Cecil last week," Tyrone answered proudly. "You ever seen anything like it, Joe Joe?"

Joe Joe shook his head in wonder. "No...never."

Tyrone slowly brought the plane down. When it landed, they both ran to look at it.

"You could get one, too," Tyrone said to Joe Joe. "We could fly them together."

"I'd love to have a plane like this. But I'd have to save for months! It's gotta cost a lot of money...."

"Just come with me and work for Cecil. He's always looking for new kids to run for him."

Joe Joe frowned at the plane. He was thinking about Cecil. He didn't even know what Cecil did, but the kids who worked for him all looked awfully tough. A lot of them were in KC's gang and in trouble at school a lot. "I don't know, Tyrone...."

"Well, just think about it. It's easy money. *Real* easy money."

Joe Joe heard his grandma calling his name. "Joe Joe! Dinner's in a few minutes!" He looked up and saw his father already walking toward the house.

"I gotta go, Tyrone."

"Right. Well, you think about what I said. Cecil pays good money."

Joe Joe glanced again at the remote-controlled plane and nodded. "I'll think about it. See you tomorrow at school."

Joe Joe washed up quickly. He sat at the kitchen table and read his library book while he waited for his dad to finish getting Brandon cleaned up.

Bessie Coleman

The beginnings of the Tuskegee Airmen can be traced to two African American pioneers in the field of aviation: Eugene Bullard and Bessie Coleman.

"I never heard of either of them," Joe Joe frowned.

Eugene Bullard left his home in Georgia and arrived in Paris, France, in 1913 looking for a better life. After the start of World War I, he joined the French Air Force. In 1917 Eugene Bullard became the first African American ever to qualify as a military pilot.

Bessie Coleman was living in Chicago in 1919 when she decided she wanted to learn to fly. Since none of the flying schools near Chicago would accept an African American student, she applied to flying schools in France. She was accepted and left for France in 1920. By June 1921, Bessie Coleman had become the first black woman in the world to earn a pilot's license.

These brave pilots knew that they were doing more than flying a plane. They were flying to prove that African Americans could become the best they could be at whatever they chose to do.

"The best they could be," Joe Joe repeated quietly and closed his book.

"It's Brandon's turn to say the blessing," Mr. Rawlings said as the rest of the family joined Joe Joe at the dinner table.

Brandon grinned and squeezed his eyes shut tightly. "Thanks to God! Amen."

"Amen," Joe Joe, his father, and grandmother echoed with wide smiles.

Cadets study a map before taking off in a training exercise. These pilots were among those who later became known as the Tuskegee Airmen.

Joe Joe turned to his father as Mr. Rawlings laid a slice of meat loaf on Brandon's plate. "What exactly does Cecil do, Dad?" Joe Joe asked. "I mean, I know he pays Tyrone a lot of money," he continued, holding out his plate to his grandmother for a serving of mashed potatoes. "And Tyrone says it's easy work."

"Joe Joe, I'm not quite sure *what* Cecil does. But from what I can tell, it's not something you should get mixed up in, no matter what he pays and no matter *how* easy the money is. In fact, Officer Joe Brown, who works this neighborhood, spoke at our block club meeting last week. He said the police are watching Cecil's house *very* closely."

"But, Dad, did you see Tyrone's plane…?"

Mr. Rawlings put down his fork and looked at Joe Joe. "Son, it's hard to explain. But we all have to make choices in life—choices between right and wrong. And the older you get, the harder it is sometimes to decide what to do."

When Joe Joe frowned, his father continued, "Starting at about your age, when I had a decision to make, my mother would sometimes say to me, 'A still small voice will speak to you and tell you which way you should go.' A still small voice, Joe Joe. Can you understand that?"

"Sounds like something from the Bible," Joe Joe answered slowly.

"Um-hum," his grandmother nodded as she looked over at Joe Joe. "From the Old Testament… the book of Isaiah, the prophet. Isaiah was telling the people of Israel that God's spirit would speak to them and tell them what to do when they had tough choices to make."

Joe Joe was quiet through the rest of dinner. But he could still hear the buzz of Tyrone's plane as he ate his meat loaf and mashed potatoes.

That night as Joe Joe lay in bed, he opened his library book and read a little more.

Before 1941 black American soldiers were not allowed to train to become military pilots. But when America entered World War II, a segregated unit—the 99th Squadron—was created for African American pilots. They were trained in Tuskegee, Alabama, and were called the "Tuskegee Airmen."

"They must have been real proud!" Joe Joe thought to himself. He wanted to keep reading, but his eyes were so tired that he fell asleep instead, his head resting on the open pages of his book.

The next morning, when Joe Joe hurried into the kitchen, his mother was standing at the table pouring milk over a bowl of cereal.

"Joe Joe," she said, smiling at him. "I was just coming to wake you up. You're going to be late for school if you don't hurry up." She put the cereal in front of him as he slid into a chair at the table.

"Are you going to work at Mr. Booth's store this afternoon?" she asked.

He had almost forgotten it was Wednesday! Joe Joe swallowed before answering. "Sure, Mama."

"Then I won't see you 'til tomorrow morning." Mrs. Rawlings leaned over and kissed him on the forehead. "Now, hurry up and get going," she urged him gently.

Joe Joe shovelled more cereal into his mouth, grabbed his book bag, and rushed out the door.

A long line of customers waited at the cash register when Joe Joe arrived at the store that day after school. As Joe Joe approached, Mr. Booth pointed to a pile of boxes, already opened in the middle aisle. "Go on and start shelving those cans, please, Joe Joe. I think you can handle them by yourself today," Mr. Booth instructed quickly.

"No problem, Mr. Booth," Joe Joe replied as he put down his things and got right to work. He couldn't believe it! Mr. Booth had never let him work by himself before. A special feeling came over him, and a glow of pride lit his face as he reached for another can.

When Joe Joe was finished, Mr. Booth walked over with an envelope in his hand. "You worked extra hard today, Joe Joe. So, I put a little something extra in the envelope for you."

Joe Joe grinned. "Thanks a lot, Mr. Booth," he said as he shoved the envelope in his back pocket and picked up his book bag.

"See you next week," Mr. Booth said and waved good-bye.

Joe Joe was still grinning as he walked home. Then he glimpsed Tyrone up ahead, dashing between two houses. Joe Joe waved and called out, but Tyrone didn't even look back. "He's probably doing something for Cecil," Joe Joe reasoned.

Joe Joe felt in his back pocket for the envelope that Mr. Booth had just given him. Then he thought about all the "easy" money he could make working for Cecil. Joe Joe walked on, but he wasn't smiling anymore. He felt confused.

At home, Joe Joe walked straight to the kitchen. No one was there. The only sound he heard was the hiss of his father's welding torch out in the garage. A plate of sugar cookies sat on the table, but Joe Joe didn't feel like eating. He walked slowly upstairs to his room, dragging his book bag behind him.

His library book about the Tuskegee Airmen was on his desk where he had left it that morning. He sat down and opened the book.

Those first Tuskegee trainees were all college graduates....

Joe Joe frowned at the page. "That's why I started working for Mr. Booth," he reminded himself. "To save money so *I* can go to college...." He kept reading.

Those first Tuskegee trainees were all college graduates. Because the Air Force's pilot training was so difficult, they knew most of America would be watching to see if they would succeed or fail. They knew that some people would look at them—and their military records—to decide if African Americans would be allowed to participate in other professions that had been closed to them. They knew they were flying for freedom not only in the war overseas, but in the battle for fair and equal treatment as African Americans at home. They were determined not to fail....

Joe Joe's reading was interrupted by the loud buzzing sound of Tyrone's remote-controlled airplane. He went to his bedroom window and saw the plane high in the sky behind his house. "I'll never be able to afford a plane like that by working for Mr. Booth," Joe Joe thought as he watched longingly. "Where is that still, small voice telling me what to do?"

Joe Joe closed his eyes and prayed out loud, "Dear God, help me to hear your voice. *Please,* help me to hear it."

This is Capt. Benjamin O. Davis in the cockpit of his training aircraft. Capt. Davis was eventually promoted to general, the first African American general in the U. S. Air Force.

The next day when Joe Joe came home from school, his grandmother was waiting for him in the kitchen. She handed him a cookie and said, "Your father is in the garage. He wants you to go out there—and bring your library book on the Tuskegee Airmen."

Joe Joe swallowed a bite of the cookie and broke into a big grin. He got his book and ran out the back door—straight to the garage. "Dad!" he called out. "What have you been working on? Let me see…."

"Hold on, Joe Joe," his father directed him as he pulled two old crates together. "Let's sit down for a minute."

Joe Joe sat down beside him and waited eagerly.

Mr. Rawlings began slowly. "I know you've been reading a book about the Tuskegee Airmen. Did you know I was about your age when I first heard about them myself?"

"Really, Dad?"

"Um-hum. There was an elder at my church, a man named Mr. Stevens…"

Joe Joe interrupted. "He was a pilot, Dad?"

"Well, no, Joe Joe. He *was* a Tuskegee Airman, but not all of the Airmen flew planes."

"Huh?"

"Mr. Stevens was an airplane mechanic. And it was after hearing Mr. Stevens talk about working on the P-40s—those old planes the Tuskegee pilots flew—that I knew I wanted to work with my hands when I grew up. When I finished high school and went to work at the factory, they offered some of us the chance to take special classes and become welders. I signed up right away. It took a while—there were a lot of classes—but I finally got my certificate."

Joe Joe quickly turned the pages of his book.

"Look, Dad! Here's a picture of a P-40." Joe Joe pointed to a page in the book. He began reading out loud…

The Air Force did not make it easy for the Tuskegee Airmen to succeed. The new pilots had to train on planes called P-40s. These were old, obsolete planes that were no longer being used by the rest of the Air Force. But even with such old equipment, the 99th Squadron did not fail. During the war, they flew more than 15,000 sorties (combat missions) and received hundreds of medals for their achievements, including more than 150 Distinguished Flying Crosses. The Tuskegee Airmen worked hard and kept their eyes on the goal because they were flying for freedom.

When Joe Joe stopped reading and looked up at his father again, Mr. Rawlings was holding something in his hand: an airplane.

"It's a model P-40!" Joe Joe exclaimed as his father handed the plane to him. He looked around at the welding equipment in the garage. "You made this for me?"

"Yes, I did," his father assured him. "Even before you brought home that book, I wanted you to know about the Tuskegee Airmen and what I learned from Mr. Stevens."

Just then, Joe Joe heard the sound of Tyrone's remote-controlled plane out in the field. But this time, the noise didn't bother him.

"Why don't you read some more?" Mr. Rawlings suggested.

Joe Joe cradled his new plane in his lap and continued…

The Tuskegee Airmen succeeded even when many others believed they would fail. Along with the other African American aviation pioneers, the Airmen helped lead the way for freedom flyers such as Lloyd Newton, the first African American pilot to fly with the Air Force Thunderbirds; Guion S. Bluford Jr., the first African American in space; Mae C. Jemison, the first African American woman in space; and Bernard A. Harris Jr., the first African American to walk in space.

The Tuskegee Airmen fought for freedom. They worked hard, and they won the battle—both for their country in the war overseas and for those African Americans at home.

Joe Joe closed the book. He looked beyond the open garage door and saw Tyrone's plane soaring high in the air. Then he looked down at his own plane—the model of the Tuskegee Airmen's P-40. Then he heard it—that still, small voice!

The voice reminded him that the Tuskegee Airmen had worked hard and become pilots. Joe Joe's own father had worked hard and become a welder. Joe Joe could *keep on* working hard at school and for Mr. Booth and go on to college and do anything else he dreamed of doing. "I *won't* take the easy way and work for Cecil!" he decided silently.

Joe Joe looked up at his dad. "Thanks for the plane, Dad!"

"You're welcome, son. You're very welcome." Mr. Rawlings beamed as Joe Joe gave him a big hug.

Above: Astronauts Mamoru Mohri and Mae Jemison aboard the space shuttle *Endeavor* as they prepare to descend from orbit.

Mae Jemison, the first African American woman in space, floating in Spacelab.

Joe Joe ran out of the garage and over to the field. "Tyrone," he called out. "Look what my dad made for me!"

Tyrone looked at Joe Joe's plane. He shrugged. "You could have one like mine, you know."

"I know," Joe Joe answered honestly. Then he added with pride, "But I'll fly my own plane—the one my dad made for me."

Then Joe Joe took his model P-40, held it high above his head, and zoomed across the field.